The Wobbly Jelly Hunt

One day, the Tweenies wanted to make something that they all liked to eat.

"Oh, can we make jelly?" asked Fizz. "I like jelly."

"Me too," agreed Milo.

"That's a good idea," said Max. "You can each have a different flavour. And we can add some fruit, too. I've got raspberries, strawberries, oranges and blackcurrants."

"Mmmm. Fruit jellies! I like the sound of those," said Jake, excitedly. The Tweenies couldn't wait to start.

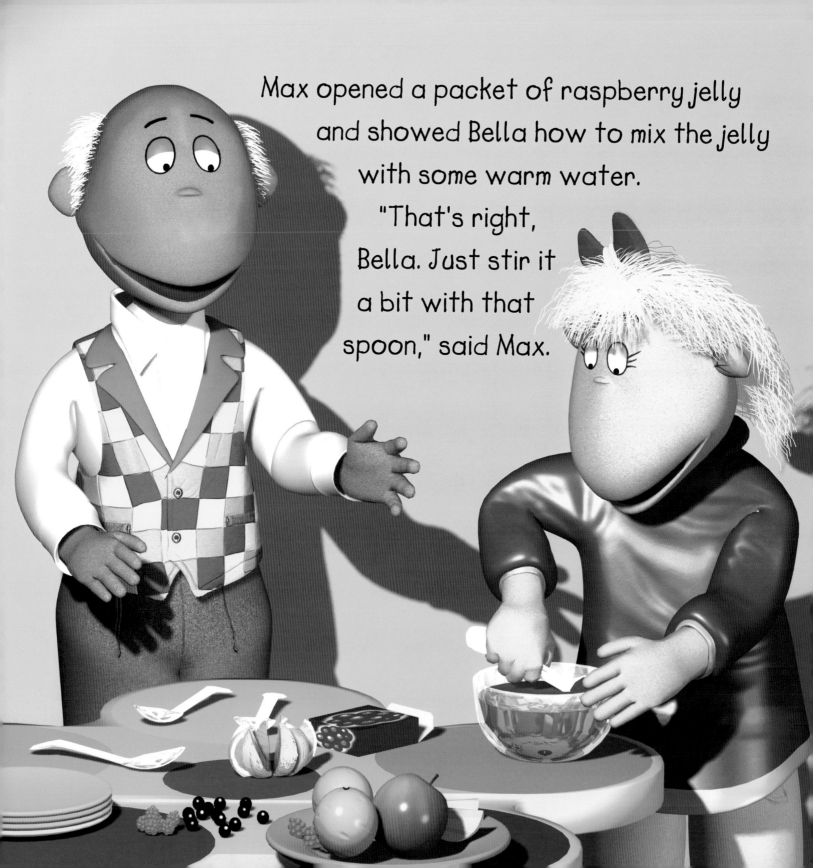

Max opened a packet of raspberry jelly and showed Bella how to mix the jelly with some warm water. "That's right, Bella. Just stir it a bit with that spoon," said Max.

"What shall
I do, Max?"
asked Jake.

"Choose a
flavour, Jake,
and I'll show you
how to make your jelly."

Jake chose strawberry
and mixed the jelly with water,
just like Bella had done.

"Oh, can I have orange
flavour?" asked Fizz, excitedly.

"I suppose I'll have to have
the blackcurrant then,
because it's the only one
left," said Milo.

Soon, the Tweenies were ready to pour the jellies into their moulds.

"Now we can add the fruit," said Max.

Bella added some raspberries to her jelly. Jake added some strawberries to his. Fizz put orange segments in her jelly and Milo sprinkled lots of blackcurrants into his.

Then Max put the jellies in the fridge.

"Mmmm, I'm hungry. Can we eat the jellies now?" asked Fizz.

"We've got to let them set first," said Max.

"But I want to taste one now!" said Bella, crossly.

"Me, too!" said Milo and Jake at the same time.

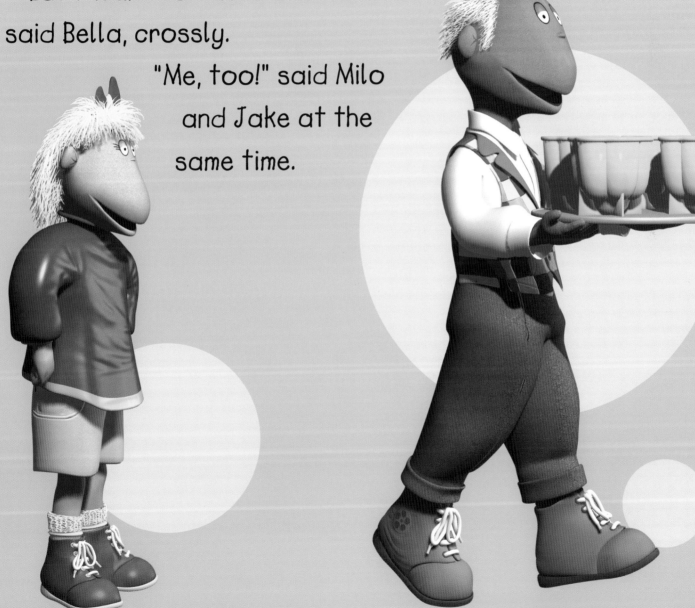

Max explained that the jellies would be soft if they tried to eat them now.

"Jelly should be wobbly, not runny," said Max.

The Tweenies looked very disappointed.

"I can't wait much longer," said Jake, rubbing his tummy.

"Neither can I," agreed Bella.

"Nor me," said Fizz.

"What can we do while we're waiting?" asked Milo with a sigh.

Then Max had an idea.

"I know," he said. "You can go on a treasure hunt!"

Max explained.

"I'm going to give you some clues and you have to find the treasure," he said with a smile.

"That sounds like fun, Max," said Fizz. "Maybe we'll find gold and jewels."

"Let's get ready!" said Milo, and the Tweenies took off their overalls while Max prepared the first clue.

Max put some big paper circles on the floor in the middle of the playroom.

"These are stepping stones," explained Max.

"You have to jump on them to cross the alligator swamp, to find the first clue. Careful – the alligators are hungry today!"

Fizz squealed as she jumped onto the first stepping stone. Milo, Bella and Jake followed.

"Ow – I think something bit me," shouted Jake.

"It's all right, Jake. There aren't any real alligators," whispered Bella. The stepping stones led into the garden.

Max told them the first clue.

"I'm very colourful and you can climb up my steps to the top. The fun bit is when you whizz down again to the bottom. What am I?"

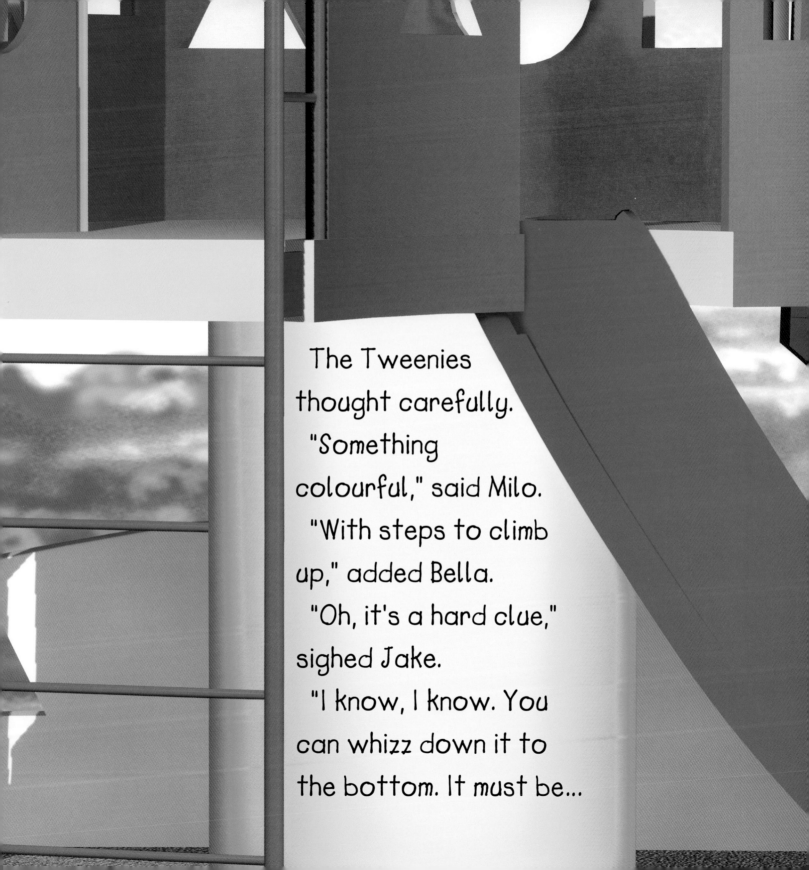

The Tweenies thought carefully.

"Something colourful," said Milo.

"With steps to climb up," added Bella.

"Oh, it's a hard clue," sighed Jake.

"I know, I know. You can whizz down it to the bottom. It must be...

...the slide on the climbing frame!" cried Fizz.

One by one, the Tweenies climbed up the steps of the climbing frame and whizzed down the slide, landing in a big heap at the bottom.

"What's the next clue, Max?" asked Milo, impatiently.

"Well," Max began. "The pink princess has been locked away at the top of the Green Tower. You have to rescue her and take her to the furry king and queen," he said, mysteriously.

"I know who the furry king and queen are," said Jake at once, spying Doodles and Izzles in a corner of the garden.

"But where's the Green Tower?" asked Fizz.

"It must be somewhere high up," decided Milo.

"Maybe the Green Tower is a...

...tree," said Bella, pointing.
The Tweenies looked up.
There, high up in one of the
trees, was a little pink doll,
wearing a pretty princess dress.

"That must be the pink princess," said Bella.

"But how are we going to rescue her? It's so high up," wailed Jake.

"Why not try working together?" suggested Max.

"I've got an idea," said Fizz. "Jake's not very heavy. Milo can give him a piggy back and then he can reach up and grab the dolly, I mean the pink princess."

So Milo crouched down and Jake jumped up on his back.
"Hold on tight," said Milo.
"Oooh, I feel a bit wobbly," said Jake.

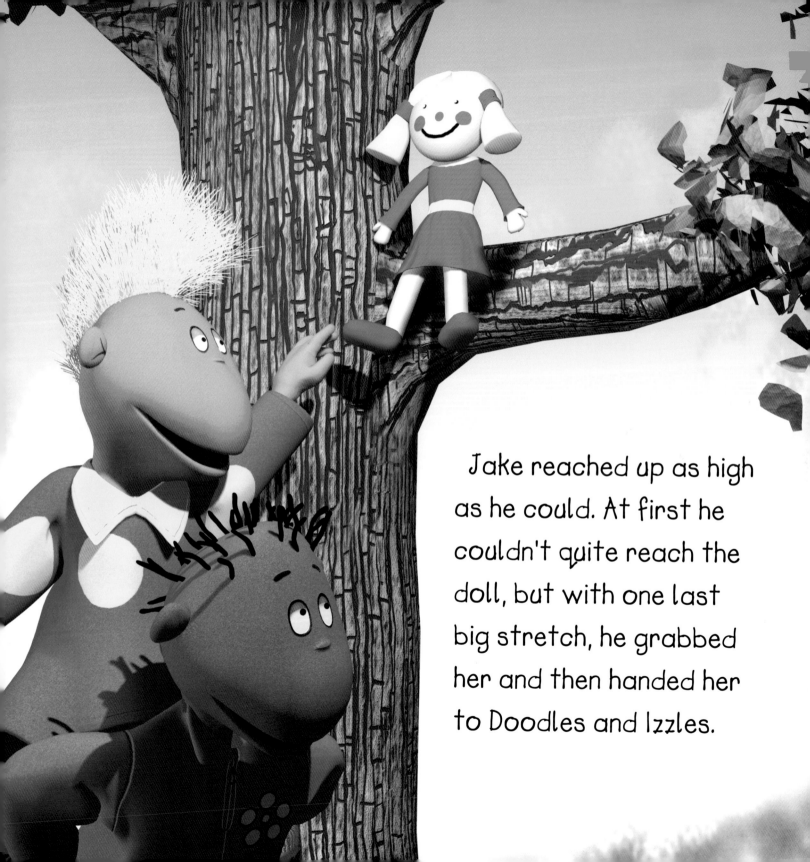

Jake reached up as high as he could. At first he couldn't quite reach the doll, but with one last big stretch, he grabbed her and then handed her to Doodles and Izzles.

"Well done," said Max. "Are you ready for your next clue, now?"

"Oh, yes," said the Tweenies, all at once.

"Well, the next one's indoors. A very important picture was broken up into little pieces by a nasty goblin. You have to put it together again."

"Lots of little pieces?" wondered Bella.

"That make a picture?" thought Milo.

"I know," said Jake, spying a box on the floor. "It's this jigsaw puzzle."

"Hey, well done, Jakey," laughed Fizz.

They set to work and soon they had put all the pieces together. It was a picture of a house.

"Where's Max?" said Bella. "We need the next clue now."

"Maybe the house is a clue," said Milo, slowly.

The Tweenies looked up and there in the window of the playhouse were Doodles and Izzles, barking excitedly.

The Tweenies ran into the playhouse and...

...there was Max with the jellies.

"You've found your treasure," Max said.

"The fruit jellies are ready now," said Jake.

"Look, they're all wobbly!" laughed Milo.

"That was quick," said Fizz.

"Time passed quickly because we were enjoying ourselves," said Bella.

"Mmmm, I like treasure hunts," said Jake.

"Woof! So do we," said Doodles and Izzles.

THE END

Caterpillar Surprise

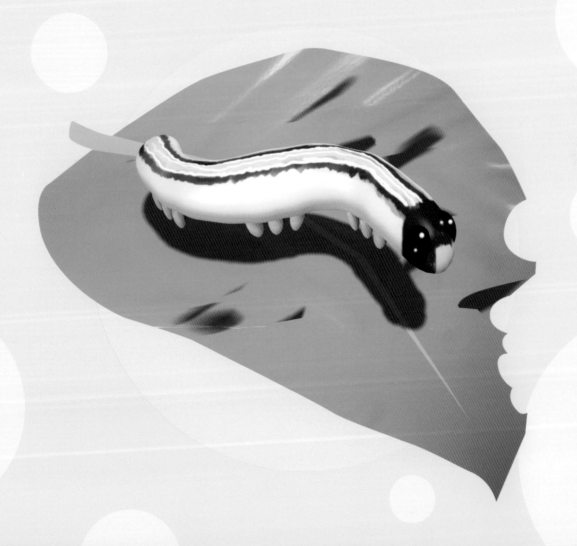

One day, Max went to visit a meadow. When he got back, the Tweenies wanted to know all about the things he had seen there.

"What did you see in the meadow, Max?" asked Fizz.

"Well, I saw some lovely wild flowers, some trees and lots of birds," Max replied.

"Did you bring anything back with you?" asked Milo.

"Do you know, I think I brought back some ants in my pants," replied Max, wriggling a bit.

That made Bella, Milo, Fizz and Jake giggle.

"What else did you see in the meadow, Max?" asked Jake.
"Did you see any tigers or elephants?" asked Milo.

"No, tigers and elephants don't live in meadows," Max explained. "But I made a video all about the bugs I saw. Shall we watch it together?"

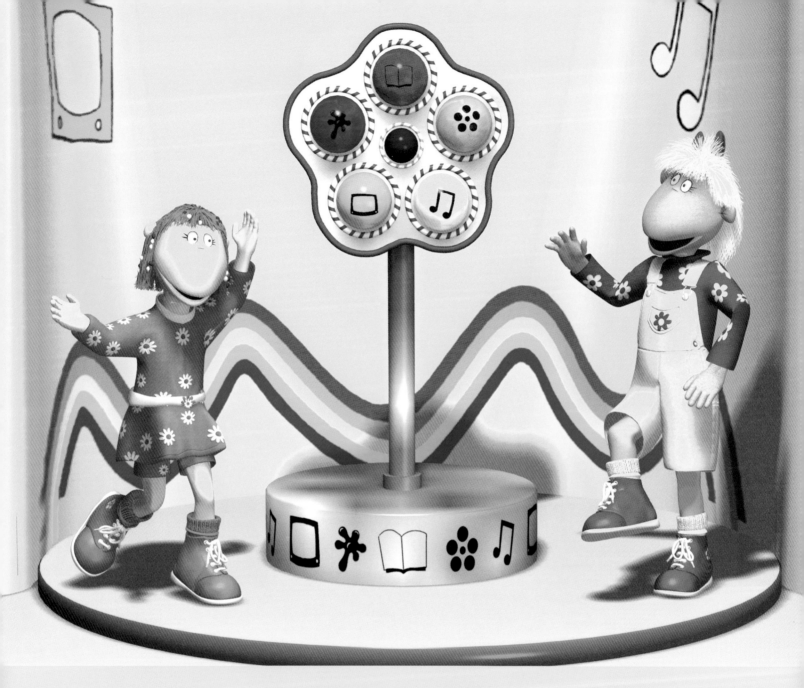

Fizz pressed the button on the Tweenie clock.

"Telly time!" she shouted.

Then they all settled down in front of the telly.

"Look!" said Milo. "There's a spider."

"That's right," Max replied. "I saw lots of spiders."

"What's that creepy-crawly?" asked Jake, looking closely at the screen.

"That's a caterpillar, Jake. What else can you see?" asked Max.

"I can see a ladybird," said Fizz.

"Did you see any butterflies?" Bella asked. "I like butterflies."

"No, I didn't see any butterflies in the meadow today, Bella," replied Max.

"Oh," said Bella sadly.

"I know. Why don't we look for bugs in the garden?" suggested Max.

"Good idea, Max," agreed the Tweenies.

The Tweenies and Max went into the garden and looked closely to see if they could spy anything crawling under the bushes or munching on the leaves.

"I can't see anything," said Milo.

"Neither can I," said Fizz. "It's just trees and twigs and grass."

"Oh, I can see something on that leaf," said Jake. "It looks like a jelly bean."

"That's not a jelly bean," said Bella. "It's a cocoon. There's a caterpillar inside it, and when it grows up it turns into something wonderful. We know a song about it... don't we, Max!"

Caterpillar walking,
Up and down the trees.

Caterpillar munching,
On the tasty leaves.

Caterpillar hiding,
Nowhere to be found.

Caterpillar sleeping,
Safe and sound.

"What happens next, Max?" asked
Milo. "Does the caterpillar wake up?"
"Well, Milo, the caterpillar does
wake up, in a way," replied Max.
"Let me explain."

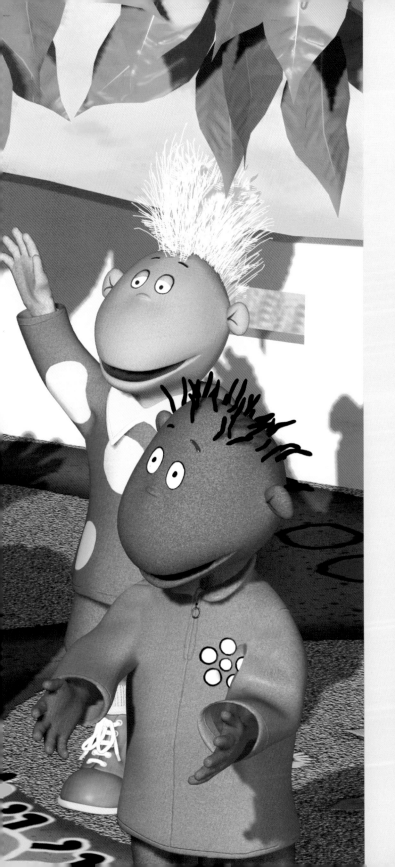

"First, a baby caterpillar grows from an egg. When the caterpillar gets bigger, it changes into something else."

"I know," said Bella. "The caterpillar changes into a..."

"Shhh, Bella!" said Max suddenly. "Let's keep the next bit a secret so that the change is a surprise."

"Can we take the cocoon inside?" asked Fizz.

"I think we should leave it here where it belongs. We can come and see it every day," replied Max.

Max went off to read the paper and the Tweenies went off to find different things to do.

Jake painted a picture of a caterpillar and Fizz drew a picture of a ladybird. Bella read a book about butterflies.

But Milo started to wonder just what was going to happen when the caterpillar woke up.

Milo went outside
and peered under the leaf
at the cocoon. He thought
he saw it move, but nothing
much else happened.

"When are we going
to get our surprise?"
he wondered.

Then Fizz went outside
to see if anything had
happened to the cocoon,
but it still looked exactly
the same.

"Where's the surprise?"
thought Fizz.

Later, Jake went outside to see if the caterpillar had woken up yet. But all he could see was the little cocoon dangling from the leaf.

"It's not much of a surprise," thought Jake.

Only Bella stayed away from the garden. She knew that you had to be patient if you wanted to enjoy this surprise. She carried on reading her book. It had some lovely pictures in it.

The next day, the day after and the day after that, there was still no sign of the caterpillar waking up. Then, early one morning, Max called Bella into the garden.

The cocoon had broken open! The outsides of the caterpillar's silky coat fell to the ground. Something small and crumpled held on tightly to the leaf.

"Oh, Max, isn't it lovely?" smiled Bella, as the small crumpled thing opened up slowly and stretched its wings.

The other Tweenies came
out to see what it was.

"Oh, it's a flutterby!" cried Jake.

"You mean a butterfly," said Fizz.

"Wow, what a great surprise!" cried Milo.

"Now we can sing the rest of the song,
Max," said Bella.

Caterpillar waking,
Looks up at the sky.

Opens out her wings,
And becomes a butterfly!

"Bye-bye butterfly!" The Tweenies waved
goodbye to the beautiful butterfly as it fluttered
away, over their heads and up, up, up into the sky.

THE END

I'm Not Scared

Bella, Milo, Fizz and Jake were having a lovely time, dancing to one of their favourite songs.

"You know you have a friend when they dance with you.
You have to choose a partner, 'cos it's better with two.

You have to spin
your partner,
that's what you do.
W-H-E-E-E-E!"

Giggling and laughing,
they spun all over the room.
"Who-aaa!" giggled Jake as
he swayed backwards
and forwards by the curtain.

Suddenly he heard a noise that made him jump!

SNUFFLE
SPLUTTER
GRUNT

"There's something behind the curtain,"
Jake cried.

"No, there isn't," said Milo. "You're imagining it."

"I really did hear something," Jake insisted.

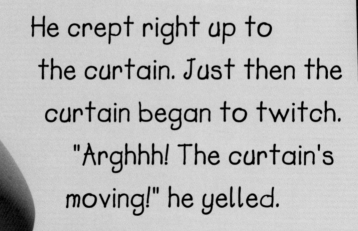

He crept right up to
the curtain. Just then the
curtain began to twitch.
"Arghhh! The curtain's
moving!" he yelled.

"You're just trying to
scare us," said Bella.

"There really really is something there," said Jake shakily.

"I'm not scared!" said Bella.

"Nor am I!" said Milo.

"We should just pull back the curtain!"
said Bella.

"Go on then, Bella,"
urged Milo.

"Why ME?" cried Bella.

"You're the oldest -
and you said you
weren't scared,"
Milo reminded her.

Bella crept slowly forwards,
but the curtain moved again.
She screamed and ran away.

"Do you think it's Max playing a trick on us?" asked Jake.

"Let's see," said Fizz. She was about to peep behind the curtain when she heard a grunting noise.

"Arghhhhh," she yelled!

The Tweenies rushed off to hide.

"There's something over there," Jake whispered. "But I'm not scared, not me!" The Tweenies decided to sing a special song to feel brave.

There's something, something over there.
But I'm not scared - no, I'm not scared.
There's something, something over there.
But I'm not scared - not me!

I hope that it's a monkey,
a monkey, a monkey.
I hope that it's a monkey
that wants to swing with me.

I hope that it's a teddy,
a teddy, a teddy.
I hope that it's a teddy that
wants to dance with me.

I hope that it's a spaceman,
a spaceman, a spaceman.
I hope that it's a spaceman
who's come to visit me.

I hope that it's a fairy,
a fairy, a fairy.
I hope that it's a fairy
to put a spell on me!

There's something, something over there.
But I'm not scared – no, I'm not scared.
There's something, something over there.
But I'm not scared – not me!

When Judy walked into the playroom,
the Tweenies **were** feeling a little braver.
"Has anyone seen my book?" Judy asked.

The Tweenies shook their heads. But when Judy walked over
to the curtain, they began to feel scared all over again.
  "ARGHHHH!" they gasped.
Judy reached behind the curtain...

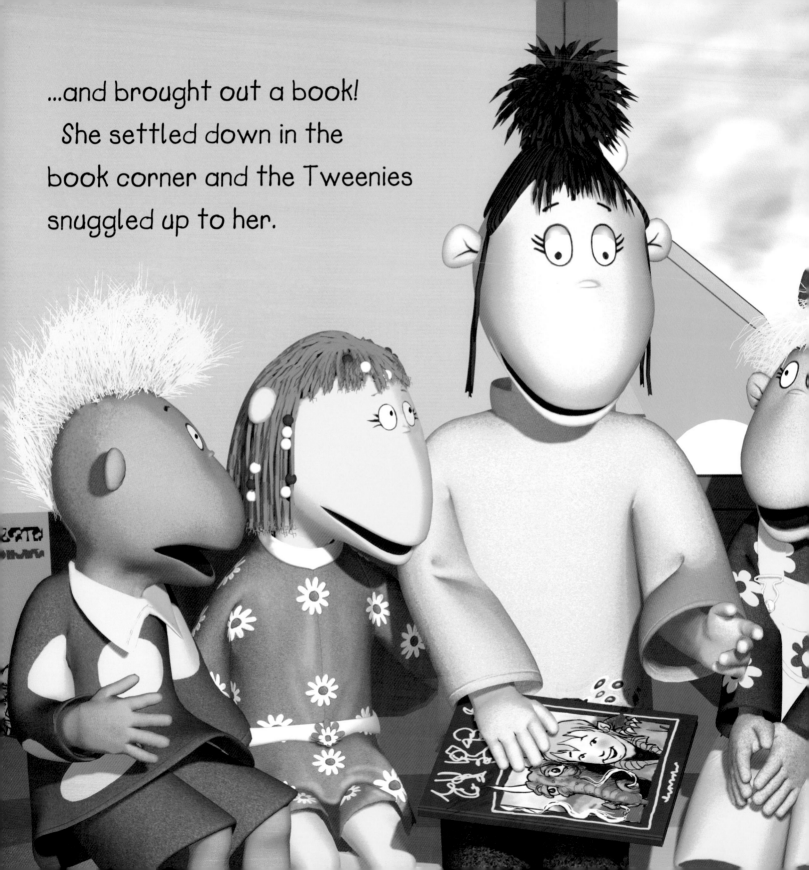

...and brought out a book!
She settled down in the
book corner and the Tweenies
snuggled up to her.

"Did you see anything behind the curtain," Milo asked.

"Yes," said Judy.

Fizz, Milo, Jake and Bella gulped.

"WHAT did you see?" squeaked Fizz.

"I saw a great, big, hairy thing," said Judy.

"Arghhhhhh!" squeaked Jake. "Has it got TEN eyes and EIGHT legs?" Judy smiled and shook her head.

"No, it's got two eyes and four legs, and it's very friendly."

"Are you sure it's friendly?" asked Fizz.

"I'm very, very sure," Judy replied. "Go and see for yourself. Don't worry. I'll be right here."

The Tweenies crept

very

very

slowly

up to the curtain.

"I'll count to three and we'll all pull together," Bella whispered.

"ONE,

TWO,

THREE,

PULL!"

"It's DOODLES!" cried Jake. "Oh, I'm so glad to see you, Doodles."

"We're not scared of Doodles," giggled Fizz.

SNUFFLE

SPLUTTER

GRUNT

Doodles woke up and wagged his tail.
"Woof! Woof!" he barked.

THE END

What Big Eyes You Have, Grandma!

One day, Max told the Tweenies the story of Little Red Riding Hood. The Tweenies enjoyed it so much they decided to do a play.

"I'll be Little Red Riding Hood," said Bella. "Fizz can be my mummy and Milo can be my daddy."

"Who can I be?" asked Jake.

"You can be my grandma," Bella told him.

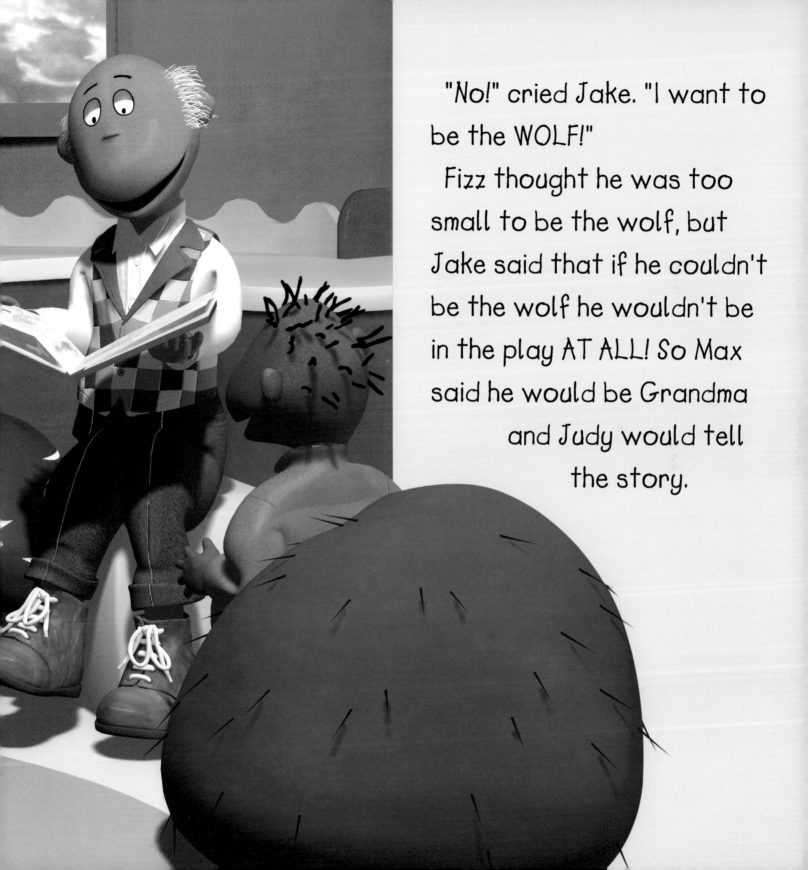

"*No!*" cried Jake. "I want to be the WOLF!"

Fizz thought he was too small to be the wolf, but Jake said that if he couldn't be the wolf he wouldn't be in the play AT ALL! So Max said he would be Grandma and Judy would tell the story.

The Tweenies rummaged through the dressing-up box for costumes. Fizz found a net curtain to wrap around herself. Jake found a fluffy scarf for a tail and made a cardboard wolf nose. Milo dressed up in a cap and coat.

"I can't find anything RED to wear!" cried Bella.

Milo suggested that she wore a blue dress, which made Bella very cross.
"I'm Little RED Riding Hood," she told him.
"Not Little BLUE Riding Hood!"

Luckily, Max found a piece of red curtain that was just right for a hood and cloak.

When Judy put some real cakes in Little Red Riding Hood's basket , Jake wanted to eat one straightaway.

"Not now, Jake," said Judy. "We're about to start our play."

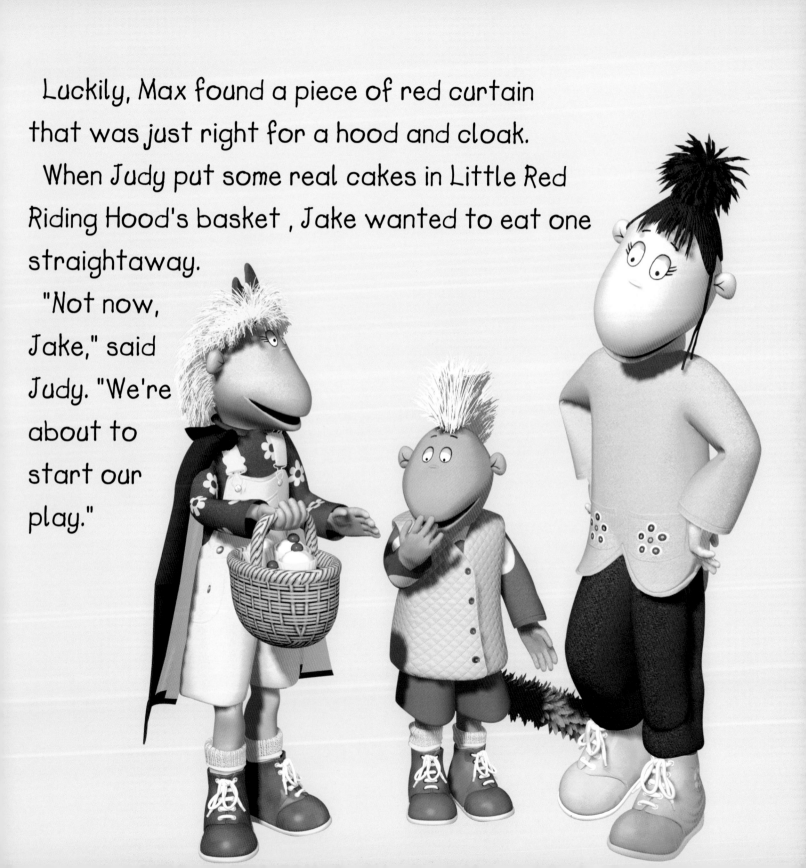

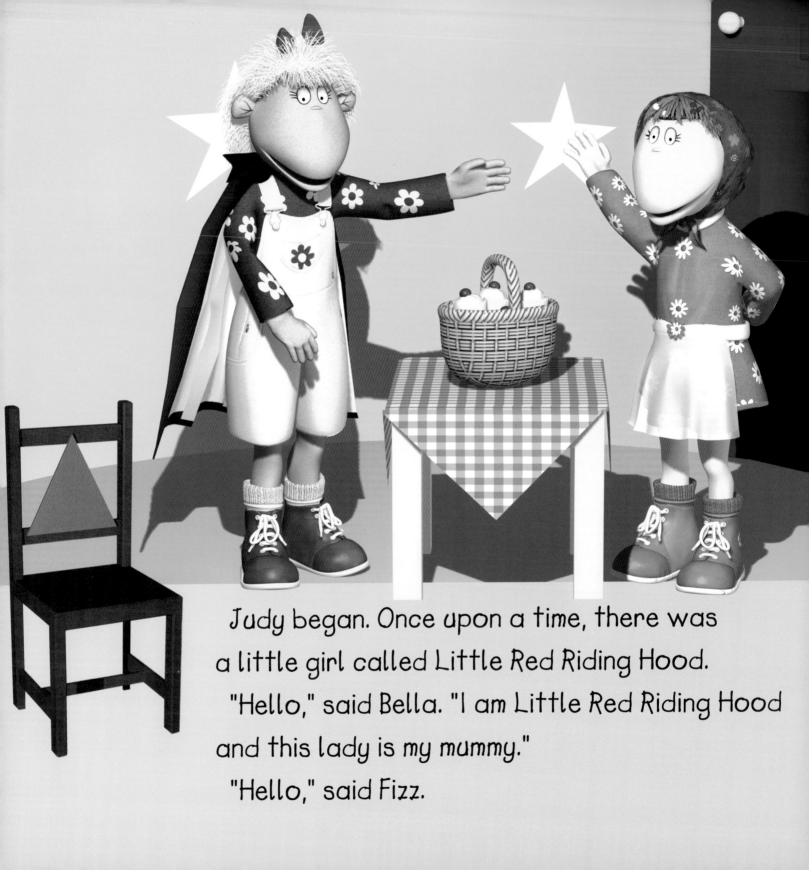

Judy began. Once upon a time, there was
a little girl called Little Red Riding Hood.
"Hello," said Bella. "I am Little Red Riding Hood
and this lady is my mummy."
"Hello," said Fizz.

Little Red Riding Hood's daddy, who'd been chopping wood in the forest, walked into the cottage.

"Hello," said Milo.

"This feather duster is my pretend axe, because real axes are dangerous."

Little Red Riding Hood's *mummy* wanted her to take a basket of cakes to Grandma, who was poorly and lived all alone in a little cottage in the forest.

"DON'T talk to anyone on the way," said Daddy.
"OK," said Little Red Riding Hood.
"I won't be long." And off she skipped.

"You've forgotten the basket," Mummy called after her.
"Oops," giggled Little Red Riding Hood. "Sorry!"

Little Red Riding Hood set off again and soon she met a wicked wolf.

"Hello," growled Jake. "I'm a friendly, big, bad, hungry, wicked wolf. Can I have one of those cakes in your basket?"

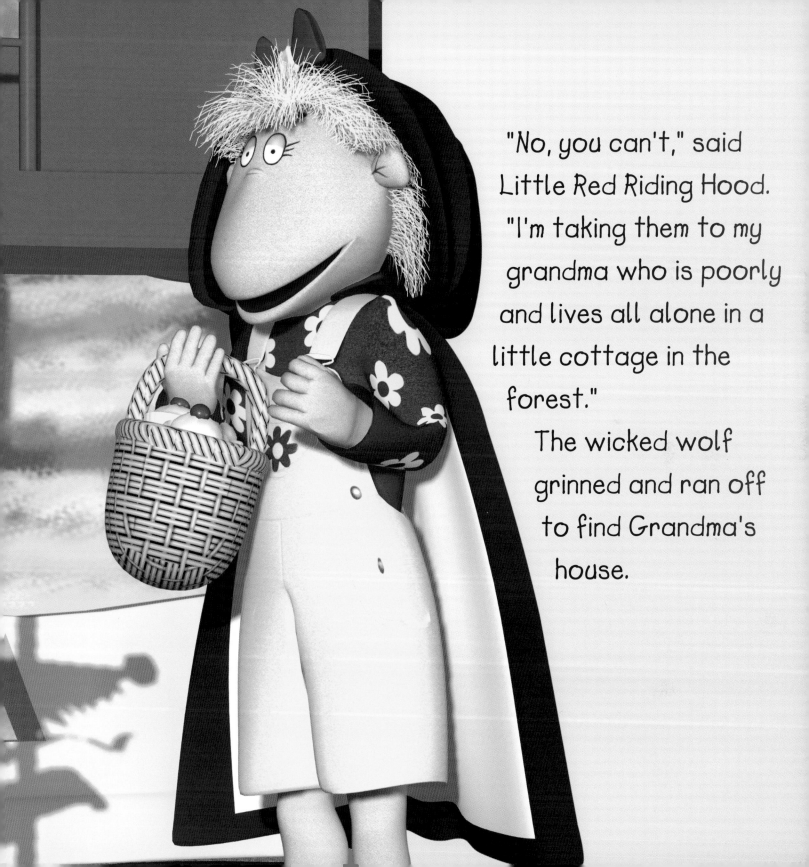

"No, you can't," said Little Red Riding Hood. "I'm taking them to my grandma who is poorly and lives all alone in a little cottage in the forest."

The wicked wolf grinned and ran off to find Grandma's house.

Grandma was in bed,
waiting for Little Red Riding
Hood. Then,
KNOCK KNOCK!

"Is that you,
Little Red Riding
Hood?" called Max,
in a special,
grandma voice.

"Yes," squeaked
the wolf.
I've brought
you a basket
of cakes."

Grandma opened the front door and...

GULP!

The wicked wolf gobbled her up in one big mouthful.

"I'm STILL hungry," thought the wolf. "I'll stay here and wait for Little Red Riding Hood."

So he put Grandma's shawl over his head and jumped into her bed.

A few minutes later, Little Red Riding Hood knocked on the door.
KNOCK KNOCK!

"Come in, my dear," squeaked the wolf.

Little Red Riding Hood STARED at her grandma.

"You're looking very furry," she said. "And what BIG EARS you have, Grandma!"

Jake couldn't remember what to say next, so Bella said it for him. "All the better to hear you with!"

"What BIG EYES you have, Grandma," cried Little Red Riding Hood.

"All the better to eat you with," squeaked the wicked wolf.

"It's not 'eat'," whispered Bella. "You SEE with your eyes!"

"Sorry," giggled Jake. "All the better to SEE you with!"

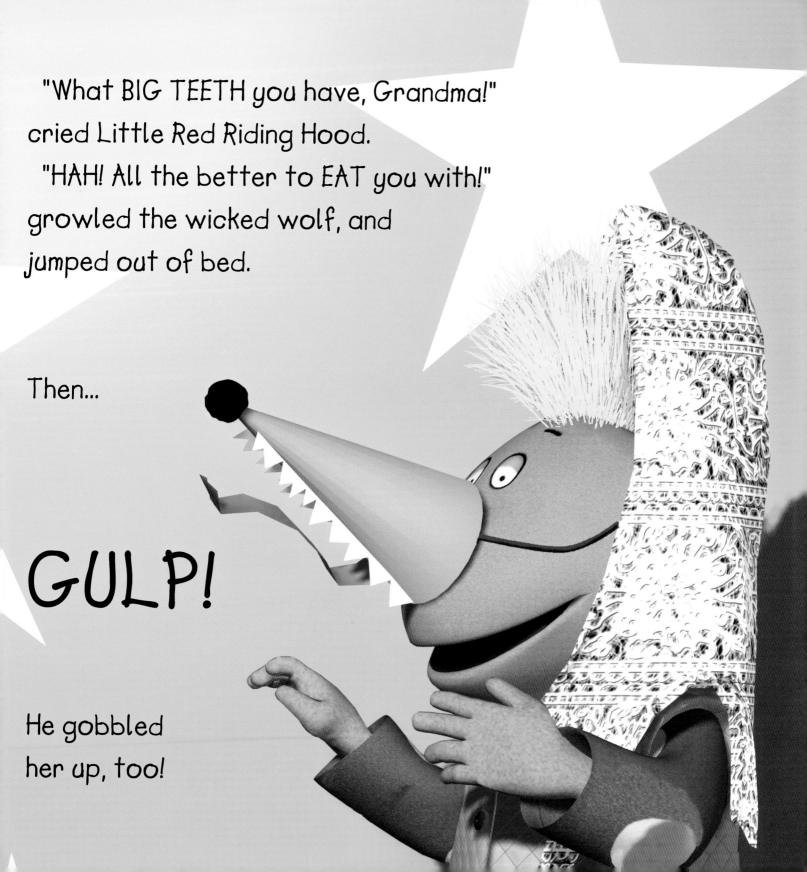

"What BIG TEETH you have, Grandma!"
cried Little Red Riding Hood.
    "HAH! All the better to EAT you with!"
growled the wicked wolf, and
jumped out of bed.

Then...

GULP!

He gobbled
her up, too!

"I'm STILL hungry," said the wolf. "I think I'll try a cake."

Just then, Little Red Riding Hood's *mummy* and daddy ran into the cottage.

"Not so fast, you wicked wolf!" cried Daddy. "I saw what you did to Little Red Riding Hood. Take that!" He whacked the wolf with his feather duster, chased him into the forest and turned him upside down.

Out popped Grandma
and Little Red Riding Hood!

"Mummy, we've been saved!" cried Little Red Riding Hood.
"You and Grandma must say 'thank you' to Daddy for
rescuing you," said Mummy. "Here he comes now."
Daddy said he'd chased the wolf out of the forest, across
the land, up a mountain and ALL the way to the moon!

"Well, we certainly won't be seeing that wicked wolf again!" said Grandma. "Now, let's eat those delicious cakes."

"So they all lived happily ever after," said Judy. "The end."

But then...

KNOCK KNOCK!

"Who can that be?" asked Grandma.

It was the wicked wolf! "I'm STILL hungry,"
he said. "Can I have a cake now?"

real
THE END

The Da Doo-Wah Woof Song!

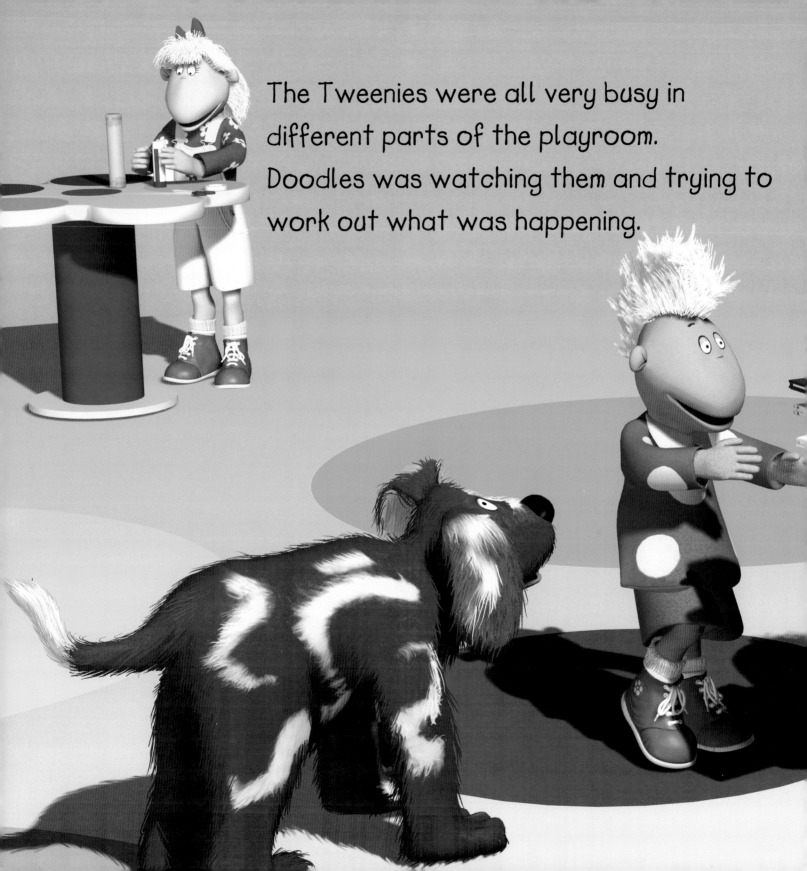

The Tweenies were all very busy in different parts of the playroom. Doodles was watching them and trying to work out what was happening.

Max walked past carrying some books.

"Better find some earplugs, Doodles," he said. "I think the Tweenies' band is getting ready to perform."

Bella was in the messy corner
making a shaker.

"Can I shake a shaker in your
band?" asked Doodles.

"Sorry, Doodles. Your paws are too clumsy to hold
a shaker," said Bella. "Try Milo."

Milo was collecting tins from the kitchen area. He was going to play the drums.

"Can I play the drums in your band?" asked Doodles.

"Sorry, mate," said Milo. "You couldn't hold the sticks in your big paws. Ask Jake."

Jake was banging two spoons together and humming.

"Can I play a spoony thing in your band?" asked Doodles.

"Sorry Doodles – your paws are too clumsy to hold the spoons," said Jake. "You could ask Fizz."

Fizz was searching for a costume in the dressing-up box. Doodles started to help her.

"Oh, Doodles – stop it!" said Fizz. "You're so clumsy. You're messing everything up."

Poor Doodles went off to find a quiet corner.
If nobody wanted him, he thought he might as
well have a snooze.

But it wasn't quiet.
The Tweenies were
starting to practise.

Doodles went over to the book
corner. It was always supposed
to be quiet there.

"Hello, Doodles!" It was Max
with another armful of books.
"Don't mind me, just
tidying up."

Doodles tried not to mind
him and closed his eyes.
But Max kept humming and
dropping books by
mistake. Doodles could not
get to sleep.

He went into the playhouse, settled down and closed his eyes.

But after a few seconds... "Bzz, bzz, bzzzzzz!" A huge fly buzzed around his nose. Doodles swiped at it but the fly came back.

Doodles decided to go into the garden. It looked quiet out there.

He was just about to lie down under the climbing frame, when...
"Plop, plop, plop." It started to rain.

Doodles looked up miserably. He had run out of places to go.

Just as he was wondering what to do, he noticed
that it had gone quiet in the playroom.

So Doodles went back inside. The playroom was unusually silent. He settled himself on a beanbag and closed his eyes.

Suddenly...

"Ladies and gentlemen. I have great pleasure in presenting to you - the Tweenies' band!"

Doodles could hardly believe his eyes. Bella, Milo, Fizz and Jake were wearing the most extraordinary costumes and singing the most extraordinary song.

Doodles is the one we all adore,
da doo-wah, woof, da doo-wah, woof.
With his floppy ears and great big paws,
da doo-wah, woof, da doo-wah, woof.

His red and yellow coat is shaggy and long,
da doo-wah, woof, da doo-wah, woof.
He's cuddly and snuggly and very strong,
da doo-wah, woof,
da doo-wah, woof.

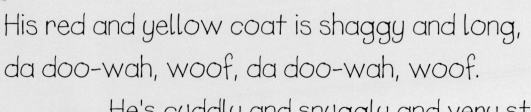

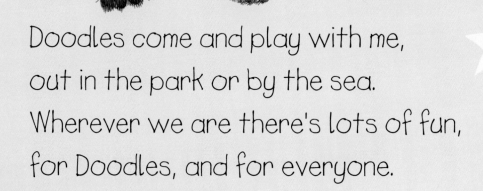

Doodles come and play with me,
out in the park or by the sea.
Wherever we are there's lots of fun,
for Doodles, and for everyone.

He likes to join in every game,
da doo-wah, woof, da doo-wah, woof.
If we listen to a story he does the same,
da doo-wah, woof, da doo-wah, woof.

We sometimes take him for a walk,
da doo-wah, woof, da doo-wah, woof.
And he's good for a chat if you want to talk,
da doo-wah, woof, da doo-wah, woof.

Suddenly Doodles didn't feel tired anymore. His paws started tapping and his head started bobbing.

Then the Tweenies sang their song again while Doodles danced and danced and danced. He even joined in with the chorus. "Woof!"

Doodles come and play with me,
out in the park or by the sea.
Wherever we are there's lots of fun,
for Doodles, and for everyone.
Yes, Doodles is the one!
Yes, Doodles is the one!

WOOF!

Now it was the Tweenies' turn to be amazed. Doodles was the best dancer they had ever seen.

He twisted and turned,

boogied and bopped,

and when the song ended he bowed for his applause.

"Oh, Doodles," said Bella. "We didn't know you could dance!" "Everyone has their own special talent, I suppose," said Fizz.

"What talent do you need to do the Da doo-wah woof dance, Doodles? Can you teach us?" asked Milo.

Doodles shook his head.

"No way!" he said. "What you need to dance like Doodles, is THESE!" And he rolled on his back and waved in the air four very big, very clumsy, very shaggy doggy paws.

THE END